# ATTERHOOD
and the Hobgoblins

  A NORWEGIAN FOLKTALE

Retold and Illustrated by
LAUREN MILLS

 LITTLE, BROWN AND COMPANY   Boston   Toronto   London

First Edition

The text for this version of "Tatterhood and the Hobgoblins" was adapted from
the original written source by Peter Christen Asbojørnsen and Jøren Moe.

Library of Congress Cataloging-in-Publication Data

Mills, Lauren A.
    Tatterhood and the hobgoblins : a Norwegian folktale / retold and illustrated by
Lauren Mills. — 1st ed.
        p.   cm.
    Summary: Tatterhood, an unconventional princess, rescues her sister from the
hobgoblins' curse.
    ISBN 0-316-57406-6
    [1. Fairy tales.   2. Folklore — Norway.]   I. Title.
PZ8.M635Tat   1993
398.2 — dc20
[E]   91-15680

The paintings in this book were done in pen-and-ink and watercolor.
Text set in Horley Old Style by Typographic House.
Display set in Colwell Handletter by Cardinal Type Service.
Color separations and printing by Princeton Polychrome.
Bound by Horowitz/Rae.

10   9   8   7   6   5   4   3   2   1

Published simultaneously in Canada
by Little, Brown & Company (Canada) Limited

Printed in the United States of America

For twins:

George & Rebecca
and
Chris & Cathy

ONCE IN THE LAND OF NORWAY THERE
lived a very rich king and queen, but for all their riches they had no
child, and this grieved the Queen greatly. She spent her hours wandering
through the empty palace halls, sighing, "If only I would bear a child, my life
would not be so lonesome and dull."

One day the Queen wandered outside the palace walls, hoping to hear the
laughter of children. As she stood near a mother playing with her young
ones, a beggar girl dressed in tattered clothing approached her. She tugged
on the Queen's sleeve and said, "If the Queen would please give me something to eat, I would tell her how she may have what she most desires."

"And how could a dirty beggar girl know the Queen's thoughts?" snapped
the Queen, smoothing out her gown where the child had touched it.

"A child of your own is what you most desire," said the beggar girl. "And
I can tell you how you may have one."

The Queen was doubtful, but she gave the beggar girl a biscuit and
listened to what she said.

"You must follow the brook yonder," instructed the child, "until you reach a wide meadow in the middle of the woods. Walk one hundred paces toward the setting sun, and there you will find two flowers. One will be very beautiful, and the other will be an ugly weed. You must eat the beautiful flower and leave the weed there. Go alone, and do not tarry. If you reach the flowers before the sun has set, no harm will befall you." And without another word, the beggar girl ran away.

Now, the Queen was afraid to enter the woods, and she was still reluctant to believe the beggar girl. She paced along the edge of the trees, wondering what to do, until her desire to have a child finally overcame her fear and doubt. Then she did as she was told—but not soon enough, for when she reached the meadow, the sun was gone, and it was the moon that lit the flowers.

The Queen recognized the beautiful flower at once and ate it. It was so delicious that she hesitated only a moment before grabbing the weed and eating *it,* too.

What could it matter? she thought. The weed was just as sweet, if not sweeter, than the beautiful flower.

"Appearances can be deceiving," she said aloud. Then she thought she heard a sinister laugh behind her. She turned quickly and saw twelve hobgoblins encircling her.

The Queen fell to her knees. "Oh, please, spare my life," she begged.

"That we will, if you give us one gift," growled the leader.

The Queen gladly agreed and began twisting her wedding ring off her finger.

The hobgoblin stopped her. "That is not the gift we want. Now, listen! You will have two daughters, for we have seen what you've done. One will be very tame and beautiful, and the other will be wild and strange. Bring the wild and strange one here to us on her twelfth birthday."

The Queen nodded her agreement. "Now be gone!" the hobgoblin yelled, and he gave the Queen a push that sent her running back to the palace faster than any bird could fly.

The hobgoblins had so frightened the Queen that she was too afraid to speak of them, even to the King. And when she discovered that she was truly going to have twins, her joy pushed the demons out of her mind altogether.

Finally the time came for the Queen to give birth. When the first daughter was born, she did not cry as any normal babe would, but giggled and exclaimed, "Mama!" when she saw the Queen.

"If I'm your mama," gasped the Queen, "may the good Lord give me grace to mend my ways!"

When the second twin was born, so fair and mild, the Queen was happy again and named the child Isabella.

As time went on, the elder twin was called Tatterhood, for she insisted on wearing a ragged, woolen cloak with a hood that hung about her ears in tatters. And as if this were not odd enough, she also rode upon a wild goat and always carried a wooden spoon with her. So different was Tatterhood from her dainty sister that it was hard to believe the two were twins and harder still to believe that Tatterhood was a princess, for she looked more like a beggar girl!

Tatterhood was a spectacle at the palace. Whether she was racing her goat atop the palace walls or crouched on her hands and knees in the mud singing to a toad, her appearance greatly disturbed the fine ladies of the court.

The Queen often tried to make Tatterhood look less wild and strange by taking away her spoon and her goat and her tattered cloak. But Tatterhood was too clever and took sport in catching her mama sneaking away with her things.

After some time the Queen gave up on Tatterhood and bestowed all her affection on Isabella. The nursemaids tried to shut Tatterhood up in a room by herself, thinking only to save their queen some embarrassment. But it was of no use, for wherever the younger twin was, there must Tatterhood be, and no one could keep them apart.

When the twins' twelfth birthday came, the Queen, remembering her promise to the hobgoblins, was full of dread as she looked upon her two daughters playing together in the garden. Fit for a queen's garden is my rose-perfect Isabella, but Tatterhood grows as wild as a weed, she thought. Yet they *both* blossom, one never harming the other. Weed or flower, Tatterhood is *mine,* and I will *never* give her up to the hobgoblins! And so the Queen celebrated her daughters' birthday with them.

But after the celebration, when the candles had long been blown out, there arose such a frightful noise in the gallery that the Queen knew the angry hobgoblins had come to fetch their due. Tatterhood ran and asked her mother what it was that dashed and crashed about so.

"Oh," said the Queen, "you wouldn't want to know."

But Tatterhood would not let up until she found out all about it, and what the Queen left out she guessed. Then Tatterhood told the King and Queen that *she* would drive out the hobgoblins. In spite of all her parents could say and however much they begged and prayed for her to leave the demons alone, she said it was *she* who must go out and drive the hobgoblins away.

Tatterhood grabbed her wooden spoon. "Keep all the doors tightly shut," she instructed, "so that not one comes so much as the *least* bit ajar. And make sure the nursemaids keep a close watch over Isabella." With that said, she sped off to fetch her goat.

Suddenly, above all the racket came a high-pitched yell and a *thud, thud, thud* and an "ouch, oooh, aagh" as Tatterhood rode through the halls whacking the hobgoblins' wicked little heads with her wooden spoon.

Now, just how it happened, no one could say, but somehow or other, in the midst of all the whacking, one of the doors did get the least bit ajar, and Isabella snuck away from her nursemaids, who all had hidden themselves under mounds of pillows. She peeked her head out of the doorway just the tiniest bit to see how her sister was getting along.

But just then, WHOOOSH! Off came Isabella's head, and on came a calf's head in its place. The hobgoblins cried out triumphantly and disappeared through the palace gates with Isabella's proper head.

When Tatterhood returned, she saw her poor sister on all fours, bellowing, "MOOOOO!"

Tatterhood shook her spoon at the irresponsible nursemaids. "And just what do you think of your heedlessness now that my sister has been turned into a calf? I suppose there is only one thing left to do if I am to set my sister free. I must go to the Island of the Hobgoblins."

Then she asked the King and Queen for a ship in full trim, well-fitted with stores, but captains and sailors she wouldn't hear of. No, Tatterhood insisted on sailing away with only her sister, and there was no use holding her back. "For after Isabella is set right, we shall sail on to see the world a bit," she said. And at last they sighed and let her have her way.

The two sailed all through the night with cold waves crashing across the deck, but Tatterhood did not tire. She steered the ship straight to where the hobgoblins dwelt, and in the morning, they dropped anchor in a misty cove.

"Stay here, Isabella, and ready the sails." Isabella nuzzled her sister's chin and mooed softly.

Tatterhood rode her goat unseen through a bog. A narrow pathway led up the rocky hillside to the hobgoblins' meeting house, and from the window she could see them celebrating. Isabella's head was on the mantle, looking very worried.

With a shrill war cry — "AIYAH!" — Tatterhood charged her goat through the open window, snapped up Isabella's head, and rode right through the other window and down the hillside.

The hobgoblins scurried close behind and surrounded her in a thick mob. Tatterhood bonked head after head with her wooden spoon while her goat snorted, butted with its horns, and kicked its hooves — until at last they were free of the horrible demons.

Isabella hoisted the sails just as the goat leapt onto the ship with Tatterhood on its back. Then *POOF!* The calf's head vanished, and Isabella stood with her proper head, just as beautiful as before. The two sisters laughed and hugged, dancing in circles, as the hobgoblins cried and stamped their grimy little feet and shook their grimy little fists all at the water's edge.

For three more years the sisters sailed to many splendid lands, but when they were finally on their way home, a fierce wind blew them off course. No matter how hard the two sisters tugged at the wheel, they could not set the ship right. The wind ripped the sails right off the masts, and they found themselves shipwrecked at the bottom of a hill in some unknown land.

Looking up the hill, they saw a magnificent castle, and charging through the gates and toward them was an army of knights!

The sisters clutched each other in fear as Isabella murmured, "And we almost made it home."

"Never mind, Isabella. I have a plan," said Tatterhood. "You stay below." With no argument, Isabella quickly slipped below deck. The knights soon gathered in front of the ship and saw only Tatterhood on her goat, dressed in her tattered cloak and riding wildly up and down the deck, her old wooden spoon in hand.

The knights had never seen anything like it and were all amazed at the sight. They asked her, "Are there more of you?"

Without stopping, Tatterhood answered, "Yes, my sister is below."

"Let us see her, too," they said.

"No. She will only be seen if the King himself comes forward," answered Tatterhood, her hair streaming behind her.

One knight boldly stepped forward. "I am the Prince and brother to the King. You may answer to me."

Tatterhood halted her goat. "My answer is: Fetch your brother if you wish to see my sister."

The other knights grumbled, but the Prince rode off to fetch his brother.

Once the King was standing in front of the ship, Tatterhood called for Isabella to come up on deck.

The King immediately fell in love with the beautiful Isabella and asked her to marry him.

Isabella herself was stricken with love but politely replied, "I could not think of marrying you unless Tatterhood marries your brother."

The crowd gasped in horror at the thought of their handsome Prince marrying such a wild thing as Tatterhood. But Tatterhood spoke up. "I will have nothing to do with marrying a prince, but I *will* ride next to him at your wedding, Isabella."

And so the wedding plans were put into action at once. Everyone in the castle was kept busy brewing and baking or sewing and stitching until, at last, the wedding day arrived. Isabella pulled Tatterhood aside. "Tatterhood, you may wear one of my dresses, if you like, and ride upon the finest horse the King owns."

But Tatterhood said, "Not I, sister. What fits you is yours. I wear my own."

There was nothing more said between the two except for wishes of well-being with hugs and kisses.

The wedding procession began. The people gathered around the bridal party as they rode from the village to the castle courtyard. Everyone marveled at the magnificence of the new bride. "Oh, isn't she just the loveliest you have ever seen?" they exclaimed. "But, uggh, what sort of bedraggled creature is her sister, who rides upon a goat and carries a silly wooden spoon? How dare she wear that ugly cloak to her own sister's wedding!"

The townspeople shook their heads and snickered, not so softly either, as Tatterhood rode past them with the Prince by her side. Tatterhood paid them no attention and neither did the Prince, as they were engaged in lively conversation. Then finally Tatterhood asked the Prince, "Well, why don't *you* ask me why I ride upon this wild goat?"

"Very well," said the Prince. "Why do you ride upon that wild goat?"

"Are you so sure it is a goat? Or might it be the grandest deer you have ever seen?" asked Tatterhood. And when the Prince looked again, the goat had indeed become the finest horned deer he had ever seen. On the saddle cloth, embroidered with silk, were all the wondrous scenes of the twins' journey.

The Prince merely smiled and nodded. They rode on a bit, this time without conversation as the Prince mused over the scenes on the embroidered cloth.

After much silence, Tatterhood asked him, "Why don't you ask me why I carry this silly wooden spoon?"

So the Prince asked, "Why do you carry that silly wooden spoon?"

"Oh? Is it a silly wooden spoon? Why it's the loveliest mahogany wand a princess ever bore!"

The Prince looked again and saw a mahogany wand such as no mortal hands had ever carved.

The Prince just smiled and nodded. They rode on a long while, speaking again in pleasant conversation as if nothing unusual had happened, until Tatterhood could stand it no longer and asked, "Well, why won't you ask me why I dress in an ugly tattered cloak and wear these weeds in my hair?"

"Ah, Tatterhood, I don't have to ask, for I know why," answered the Prince.

Tatterhood tried to wait patiently for the Prince to explain, but he remained silent. "Well, why is it, then?" she finally asked.

"You wear them simply because you have chosen to. You have the power to appear however you wish. When you *want* to look like a beautiful princess, you *will*. But only when *you* are ready. So, you see it matters very little what anyone else thinks," said the Prince.

This time it was Tatterhood who smiled and nodded. The Prince looked again at her and saw the most magnificent princess he could ever have imagined. Nestled in her hair were fragrant and exotic wildflowers, and she was wearing a most extraordinary woven cloak. Twisted in the yarns was a peculiar flower in full blossom.

"I am breathless," said the Prince, "for you are indeed the most marvelous creature I have ever known."

Tatterhood replied, "Well, for a prince, I suppose you are a most marvelous creature yourself!"

He laughed. "Ah, then you *might* have something to do with marrying a prince such as I?"

"Yes, of course," Tatterhood answered, for she did not doubt her heart. And the two were also wed that very day.

And after much festivity, both couples set out for the twins' old kingdom to celebrate anew. The Queen at first did not recognize Tatterhood, in which Tatterhood took much delight, teasing her mother that she did not know her very own daughter. The King was overjoyed to have both of his daughters wedded to such fine men. He exclaimed that Tatterhood would rule after him.

So, in time, Tatterhood ruled, fair and wise, and she and the Prince had many laughing children who filled the palace halls.

And today, out in the middle of a meadow grow two flowers. One is very beautiful, and the other is odd. On the outskirts of the nearby village awaits a beggar girl . . . for the next queen who wishes for a child.